My Mountain Song

by
Shutta Crum

illustrated by
Ted Rand

Clarion Books
New York

Clarion Books · a Houghton Mifflin Company imprint · 215 Park Avenue South, New York, NY 10003
Text copyright © 2004 by Shutta Crum · Illustrations copyright © 2004 by Ted Rand
The illustrations were executed in watercolor. The text was set in 15-point Opti Basker Ville.

www.houghtonmifflinbooks.com
Printed in Malaysia
Library of Congress Cataloging-in-Publication Data
Crum, Shutta. · My mountain song / by Shutta Crum ; illustrated by Ted Rand.   p. cm.
Summary: One summer day on her great-grandparents' Kentucky farm, a squabble with her cousin Melvin
spurs Brenda Gail to begin choosing the moments that will become her own special song made of memories.
ISBN 0-618-15970-3
[1. Songs—Fiction. 2. Grandparents—Fiction. 3. Cousins—Fiction. 4. Mountain life—Kentucky—Fiction.
5. Farm life—Kentucky—Fiction. 6. Kentucky—Fiction.] I. Rand, Ted, ill. II. Title.
PZ7.C888288 My 2004 · [Fic]—dc22 · 2003012008

TWP 10 9 8 7 6 5 4
4500367851

For my parents, Melvin and Evelyn Crum,
who had the good fortune to be born and raised in the mountains
—S.C.

To my grandson Roy Willis, who is growing up with chickens
—T.R.

In the mountains down south, morning is musical.

Moses, the rooster, wakes us with his cry from the top of Munson's Rock. My great-grandparents, Big Ma and Gran Pap, clink about the kitchen, whispering. The screen door swishes open and snaps closed. And I can hear the chickens in the yard greeting each other, cackling and scolding.

Then I hear Gran Pap's voice. "Brenda Gail! You up yet, sleepyhead?"

"Coming!" I jump out of bed, hug Duke, and pull on my overalls. This is my first summer here all by myself, without a little brother tagging along or a big brother telling me what to do.

We go to the henhouse, just Gran Pap, Duke, and I, to collect eggs. Gran Pap slides his long knobby hands down in the shallow nests, pulls out eggs, and gently lays each one in the blue bowl I carry. I can hear him singing under his breath.

"What's that you're singing?" I ask him.

"Just my mountain song," says Gran Pap.

"Your mountain song?" I ask. "What's that?"

"Mine's a real old song," he answers, moving little Dolly off her nest. "It's made out of bits and pieces, like one of your great-grandmother's quilts. It's got good memories in it—like meeting her when she was a young girl, and drinking cold spring water after we've just brought it down the mountain. Everybody born in the mountains got a song inside them."

"They do?" I ask. "What about Big Ma?"

"Yup, she's got one."

"What about me? I was born here, too," I remind Gran Pap. "What about *my* song?"

"You've got one," says Gran Pap. "It's just waiting to come out. You'll find it by thinking about things you like about the mountains and putting them all together."

I look down at the blue bowl. We have nine eggs so far. "Can I put gathering eggs with you and Duke in my song?" I ask.

He takes an egg out from under Morning Glory, Big Ma's favorite hen, and says, "I'd like that a lot."

"I can put Morning Glory in it, too," I say. "She's the prettiest hen and the best mama."

"I expect she'd be pleased," says Gran Pap. He tips his hat to her, and I giggle. Gran Pap always treats Morning Glory like a lady.

Now my pesky cousin Melvin comes jumping over the creek that flows through the bottom and starts up the path. "Hey, Shuck Beans! Pap!" he yells.

"My name ain't Shuck Beans!" I shout back. "Pap, I don't have to put Melvin in my mountain song, do I?"

"You don't have to put anything in you don't want in," Gran Pap says.

Melvin spends most of his time at Gran Pap's house when anyone's visiting, so I knew I'd have to put up with him this summer. But I was hoping to have Big Ma and Gran Pap to myself, at least for my first whole day.

"Hey there, Dog Dust," Melvin says, stopping to scratch Duke's head.

If Gran Pap hadn't been right there, I'd have whomped Melvin for sure, even though he's bigger'n me. "My dog's name is *Duke*," I say with clenched teeth, and head for the house.

Big Ma's got potatoes,
and biscuits and gravy, ready.
There's sliced tomatoes, homemade
jam, and cold fresh milk, too. I put the
bowl of eggs down on the counter, wash my
hands, and sit at the table. Gran Pap and Melvin
are right behind me.

As I eat, I wiggle my bare toes back and forth in Duke's warm
fur and think about my mountain song. I tug at Gran Pap's shirt. "I
think I'll put Big Ma, cooking up breakfast, in my song," I whisper.

Gran Pap leans over and whispers back, "She's a-cooking in mine, too!"

Later, Melvin and I go down to the bottom with Gran Pap to dig early potatoes. Gran Pap lifts the mounded soil with his garden fork. Then Melvin and I come along behind him and dig in with our hands, racing to see who can uncover the most. We can hear Gran Pap's high singing voice as he works his way toward the far end of the potato patch.

"What's Pap singing?" Melvin asks.

I sit up and listen for a moment. I smile. "It's just a song," I tell him.

"I know a song," Melvin says. He jumps up and starts caterwauling, "I been workin' on the railroad—"

"It ain't that kind of song!" I shout. He stops his racket and frowns at me. I roll my eyes at him. "It's a special song."

"What do you mean, a special song?"

"If you must know, it's Gran Pap's own song about special things, like the mountains and people he likes and such. He told me all about it himself. He says Big Ma's got one also. And I'm going to have one."

"I got one, too," says Melvin.

"No, you don't."

"Yes, I do!"

"No, you don't. 'Cause I just now told you about them. So there!" I tell him.

"I bet any song you make up will be too stupid to sing," says Melvin.

"Oh, yeah?" I say. Now he's got me really mad. "You know something? You're always spoiling everything by hanging around here!"

"Well, I ain't *ever* putting you, or that pile of dog dust, in any song of mine!" Then Melvin backs up and kicks dirt at me!

"That's fine with me! And quit calling him *Dog Dust*—his name is Duke!" I yell. As Melvin turns and stalks away, I grab a handful of dirt and stones and throw them at his back.

Just then, Morning Glory comes pecking around the end of the potato patch—and right into the shower of stones. Suddenly, she's lying on her side.

"Oh, no!" I scream, and run to her. "Oh, no, no!"

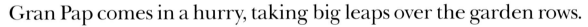

Gran Pap comes in a hurry, taking big leaps over the garden rows.

"Morning Glory!" I cry. She's staggering and flopping around, trying to get up and falling back down. "Oh, Morning Glory. I'm so sorry. I didn't mean to hurt you!"

Gran Pap bends down and quickly examines her

"Oh, Gran Pap! I didn't mean to hurt her, Pap!" Now I can hardly see for the tears washing down my face.

"I know. I know," Gran Pap says.

I bury my face in my hands. "I can't look! How hurt is she?"

Then I hear Melvin's voice. He makes me feel even worse. "Is she dead?" he whispers. "Big Ma's gonna go plumb crazy."

I look up as Gran Pap carefully lifts Morning Glory in his big hands. "I think she's gonna be all right," he says. "We'll see."

18

19

Melvin and I follow Gran Pap back to the house. Big Ma's out on the porch. "Mercy!" she groans, and clutches at her apron. "What happened to Morning Glory?"

No one answers Big Ma, but they all stand looking at me.

Finally, Gran Pap pipes up, "Now, don't take on so, Jennie Belle. Morning Glory's gonna be fine. You got your clothes basket right handy?"

When Big Ma returns with the wicker basket, Gran Pap lays Morning Glory in it. "Look. I think she's coming around."

Big Ma leans over to run the tip of her finger along the side of Morning Glory's head. "You poor little thing," I hear her whisper. Then she straightens up and asks again, "What happened?"

I'm almost afraid to look at Big Ma, but I do. "I'm sorry," I say, wiping my arm across my eyes and my nose. "I was throwing rocks at Melvin." I hang my head. "I didn't mean to hit Morning Glory."

Big Ma takes a good hold of my chin and tilts my head up. "I know you didn't mean to hurt her," she says, looking me right in the eye. "But you know better than to throw rocks."

"Yes'm." I sniff.

"Go on in and sit in the corner. I don't want to set eyes on you till supper. You hear?"

"Yes'm."

"And you, young man," Big Ma says to Melvin, "you git on and help your gran pap with his chores."

I sit in the front room with Duke. I stare at the linoleum and think about how Morning Glory's gonna be in my song so she's *gotta* be all right.

I have Morning Glory, and Gran Pap collecting eggs, and Big Ma cooking, and Duke to put in my song. I trace my finger around and around the yellow flowers on the floor. And then a little bit of song comes to me, and I close my eyes and start to sing.

After a while, Melvin brings me a sandwich. "Here," he says. "Big Ma said to bring you some lunch. I made it myself."

I lift the top slice of bread and peek in to be sure it's OK to eat.

"It's just butter and Big Ma's strawberry jam," he says. He's got jam all around his mouth.

I take a big bite. "Thanks."

"Morning Glory's been walking around a little," Melvin says.

"That's good," I say.

"Gran Pap says she got stunned a bit." He kind of clears his throat. "And he said I had to apologize for kicking dirt at you. Besides," he goes on, "you were right. I don't have my song yet. Gran Pap says I have to make it up as I go along. So…"

"So?"

"So I was thinking about putting you and Dog Dust—um, your dog—in my song," he says. "That is, if it's all right with you."

I can hardly believe it. Melvin is actually trying to be nice! "His name's *not* Dog Dust," I remind him.

Melvin bows low to Duke. "His Highness, the *Royal* Duke of Banner Mountain!" Then he laughs. "I know," he says. "We can make him a crown."

"Yeah!" I say. Maybe it won't be *so* bad to have Melvin around. "I'm sorry, too. About throwing rocks at you."

"What about your song, Shuck Beans?" Melvin asks. "Am I in it?"

"Maybe. But my name ain't Shuck Beans."

"Oh, all right, Miss Brenda Gail Munson." Then he quickly up-ends, stands on his hands, and crashes to the floor. That's when Duke jumps up and starts licking his face. His Royal Highness likes Big Ma's jam, too!

27

28

After supper, we all go out on the long front porch to watch Melvin run home. I can hear Big Ma singing softly to herself. I try to catch some of her song.

She shakes her head and smiles. "That Melvin," she says. "He's just like Gran Pap when he was a boy."

"He is?" I look at Gran Pap.

He winks at me.

"Tomorrow," I say to Big Ma, "can we go up the mountain to get spring water?"

"Just me and you?" she asks. "No boys?"

"No boys," I say, and I hear Gran Pap laugh out loud.

"I can't wait," she answers. Then she says, "I've always loved summer here in the mountains."

"Me, too!" I tell her. And I know this moment will be in my song.

Later, raindrops plip-plop lightly on the tin roof. "Summer rain," Gran Pap says.

All around us is the sweet-smelling dark. "Gran Pap," I ask, "how do I get a good smell into my song?"

Gran Pap rocks in the old applewood rocker and scratches his head. After a bit, he says, "Now, that's something I've been studying on for years, Brenda Gail. But I haven't rightly figured it out. If you'll help me work on it, we can put it in both our songs."

"I will!" I tell him. And I turn to the summer night and breathe in deep.